Piper's GREAT Adventures

MARK LOWRY
AND MARTHA BOLTON
Illustrated by Kristen Myers

HOWARD
PUBLISHING CO.

Piper's Great Adventures © 2005 Mark Lowry
All rights reserved. Printed in China
Published by Howard Publishing Co., Inc.
3117 North Seventh Street, West Monroe, Louisiana 71291-2227
www.howardpublishing.com

05 06 07 08 09 10 11 12 13 14   10 9 8 7 6 5 4 3 2 1

Nighttime Is Just Daytime with Your Eyes Closed
Text Edited by Chrys Howard
Illustrated by Kristen Myers
Digital Enhancement by Tribe Design

Music by Greg Nelson and David Hamilton
Orchestrated by David Hamilton
Produced by Greg Nelson
© 1999 Word Music/ Gentle Ben/ Dayspring Music

Piper's Twisted Tale
Illustrated by Kristen Myers
Digital Enhancement by LinDee Loveland

Music by Ted Wilson
Produced and Orchestrated by Ted Wilson
Music © 2001 Gotta Believe in Music

Piper Steals the Show!
Illustrated by Kristen Myers
Digital Enhancement by Vanessa Bearden

Music by Ted Wilson, David Hamilton, and Greg Nelson
Produced and Orchestrated by Ted Wilson
Theme Music © 2000 Word Music/ Gentle Ben/ Dayspring
Other Music © 2000 Gotta Believe in Music

Piper's Night Before Christmas
Illustrated by Kristen Myers
Digital Enhancement by Suzanne Floyd, LinDee Loveland, and Vanessa Bearden

Music by Greg Nelson and David Hamilton
Orchestrated by David Hamilton
Produced by Greg Nelson
© 1998 Word Music/ Gentle Ben/ Dayspring

ISBN 1-58229-474-7

Contents

Mark Lowry is a multitalented artist, performer, and humorist, as well as a best-selling author of children's books. His lyrics to the song "Mary, Did You Know?" have been sung by more than thirty different artists, including Kathy Mattea, Kenny Rogers, Wynonna Judd, Natalie Cole, and Donny Osmond. Mark's unique presentation has been featured on more than sixty Gaither Homecoming videos, and his talent has taken him around the world to encourage those who are children of God to stay strong and to inspire those who do not know Christ to seek Him.

Martha Bolton is the author of fifty books of humor and inspiration, including *The "Official" Friends Book*, *The "Official" Hugs Book*, *The "Official" Mom Book*, and more. She was a staff writer for Bob Hope for more than fifteen years and has received both an Emmy nomination (for outstanding achievement in music and lyrics) and a Dove nomination (for *A Lamb's Tale*, a children's musical). Martha has written for such entertainers as Phyllis Diller, Wayne Newton, and Jeff Allen and is also known as the Cafeteria Lady for *Brio* magazine.

Kristen Myers is a dedicated Christian, proud mother of four, loving wife, and a gifted artist. She has several illustrated books and a greeting-card line to her credit. She lives in West Monroe, Louisiana, where her life is filled with the constant teaching that goes with parenting and the ceaseless learning that comes with being a child of God.

BOOK 1

Nighttime Is Just Daytime with Your Eyes Closed

MARK LOWRY

Illustrated by Kristen Myers

Down through the valley and just past the trees
Where the red robins ride on a warm summer breeze
And the lilacs and lilies bloom under blue skies
Is a place full of adventure and sweet lullabies.

In a small tiny village, much like your own,
Lives Piper the mouse in Piper's mouse home.
And the name of the town? It is none other than Cheddar.
No mouse could have chosen a name any better.

Well, Piper was hyper,
as everyone knows.
Piper was hyper from his
head to his toes—

Even when moonlight and stars came to play
And he had to lie down at the end of the day.

Energy oozed from his every pore,
With a mind full of questions and daydreams and more.
His head would be still, but, oh, how his mind
Would dance through the galaxies, one at a time.

Sleeping was fine
    for the rest of his kin.
He'd hear Grandpa snore
    from his chair in the den.
His brothers and sisters,
    they needed their rest,
And his mom always said,
    "Sleep can rest you the best."

But Piper would toss, he'd Y A W N, and he'd squirm...

He'd wiggle and jiggle like a little brown worm...

He'd flip and he'd flop...

So, Papa told Piper of a land far away,
Where little mice play in the heat of the day.
"Far around the world, clear out of sight,
The sun is still shining, while here it is night.

God knows how you little mice like to play,
So He invented a way to turn night into day."

Piper sat up in bed with his eyes wide open.
This was the very thing for which he'd been hopin'.

Piper told Papa, "How great that would be!
I could jump over rivers or climb up a tree.
If I could go there, wouldn't that be the best?
Then all of you could get plenty of rest."

"I'm speaking of dreamland—you don't want to miss it—
For marv'lous adventures await all who visit.

You can fly over mountains...

or breathe under sea.

"Why, you can eat fifty burgers at once if you please."

His mind began filling with possible dreams;
His head was now spinning with adventurous schemes.
And before very long, before Piper knew it,
He fell fast asleep; there wasn't much to it.

He dreamed a deliciously colorful dream—
Red lollipop treetops and blueberry streams.
Houses of chocolate with frosting on top,
Whose chimneys were stuffed with banana gumdrops.

The air smelled like hot, buttered cinnamon toast,
And the birds sang sweet songs as they winged toward the coast.
The grass at the playground was purple, not green,
And the pond at the park had a bubble machine!

Then Piper decided he wanted to fly,
So he stretched out his arms and aimed toward the sky.
With a jump and a kick, ol' Piper was soaring.
"This is fun," he exclaimed, "and not a bit boring!"

He flew past his schoolyard and over his friends.
He waved to his teacher as he swooped by again.
He decided to fly with his tail all a-curled;
He decided to fly clear around the world.

Past islands, past valleys, past mountains and streams,
He flew past Hawaii—what a wonderful dream!

With the ocean below him, he continued his flight;
He flew out of nighttime right into daylight.

He landed in China; it seemed he'd been hurled
As quick as a blink, clear around the world.
Papa was right; the sun was still shining.
He was startled to hear a mouse who was whining.

"I don't wanna nap," the little mouse said.
"I know you don't, Son, but it's time for bed.
God gave us this time so our bodies can grow
And our minds can remember the things we should know."

Piper wanted to tell him
 we all need our rest
And how Mama had said,
 "Sleep can rest you the best."
But his eyelids got heavy,
 and he nodded his head,
And his hyper heart wished
 he was home in his bed.

The sunlight had crept through a hole in the tree.
He opened one eye—waiting to see—

Was he still in the air...

...or was he in China?

Was he under his covers...

...or in south Carolina?

But Piper was still at home in his bed.
And somehow his nightcap was still on his head.
And morning had come, another new day.
His family was up; he had something to say.

"I've spent the night dreaming such wonderful dreams.
It felt just like playing, even better, it seems.
I have to admit it. Papa, you're right.
Dreams are a fun way to get through the night."

And just as God created the day,
He created the night in His own special way.
There's a lesson for us, and here's how it goes,
Nighttime is just daytime with your eyes closed.

"The Lord gives sleep to those He loves."
—Psalm 127:2

32

BOOK 2

Piper's Twisted Tale

MARK LOWRY
AND MARTHA BOLTON
Illustrated by Kristen Myers

"I'm off to the store,"
Piper's mom said one day.
"You stay right here
And just quietly play."

"Uncle Sylvester
Is taking a nap,
So stay out of trouble
Till I can get back!"

GOD BLESS OUR HOME

Love
one
another

Do not
Lie
to each
other

"Mother," said Piper,
"I'll stay in the den
And just watch TV."
And he meant it, but then . . .

His hyperactivity
Hit like a train!
All sorts of ideas
Popped into his brain!

He called up a friend
And asked if he'd come,
But six mice showed up
By the time he was done!

String Cheese brought pizza.
Cheeseball brought the chips,
And each one took turns
Diving into the dip!

Four quarters of football
And basketball too!

Soccer and baseball!
What didn't they do?

They skied down the stair rails,
Skateboarded the hall.
Poor Uncle Sylvester
Just slept through it all!

They played and they munched.
They munched and they played.
Oh, what a terrible
Mess they all made!

Then all of a sudden
They heard a mouse van
Pull up to the house,
And Piper's friends ran.

They left Piper there
To endure all the shame,
Take all the punishment,
And get all the blame.

Word has it the gasp
Piper's mom gasped that day
Could be heard in the mountains
Two counties away!

"Piper!" she said.
"What on earth happened here?"
She wanted the facts.
That fact was quite clear.

48

Piper thought for a moment
'Bout all of the fun
He'd had with his friends
And the damage they'd done.

Yet he knew if he told her,
She'd ground him for weeks.
So he made up a story,
But it had a few leaks.

"First came a *tornado*,"
Piper said, "strangest sight!
It whirled through the house,
Then it called it a night!"

"An earthquake came next

And an avalanche too!"

"Then two marching bands
Came parading right through!"

Piper spun him a tale
Like no tale you have heard,
And his tail turned and twisted
With every false word.

You see, that's what happens
To mice when they lie.
But Piper ignored it
And simply replied,

"Did I happen to mention
That NASA dropped in
To test a new rocket
Right here in our den?"

"A circus came next,
But what could I say?
Have you ever tried
Shooing lions away?"

While he made up his story—
The wheres, whens, and whats—
Piper's tail kept on twisting
In hundreds of knots.

His mother said, "Son,
That's some tale for a mouse.
Are you sure that all happened
Right here in our house?"

"It really did happen!
It's true," Piper said.
"Thank goodness that I was
Asleep in my bed."

Piper covered his tail
So his mom wouldn't know
That the tale he was spinning,
Well, it wasn't quite so.

"Now, son," she repeated,
"If you're sure that is all,
Then why are there skateboard
Tracks lining the hall?"

"Why did I see your friends
Leaving from here?
And why is there cheese dip
On our chandelier?"

Piper started to sweat,
And he turned a bright red.
If only he'd told her
The whole truth instead.

His tail was in knots!
He was sorry he lied!
But only the truth
Could now get it untied.

Piper knew that confessing
Was what he should do.
And telling the truth was
What God wanted too.

So standing up tall,
Piper laid out the facts
And said he was sorry
For his thoughtless acts.

It took him four days
To clean all the mess,
But he sure felt better
Once he had confessed.

Piper learned that he should have
Obeyed his mom first,
And lying will always
Just make matters worse.

63

Now Piper can smile,
For inside he feels GREAT!
And his tale and his tail
Are now PERFECTLY STRAIGHT!

BOOK 3

Piper Steals the Show!

MARK LOWRY
AND MARTHA BOLTON
Illustrated by Kristen Myers

THE CIRCUS IS COMING!

The banners were posted
all over the town!
The circus was coming
with monkeys and clowns . . .

And tigers and lions
    and elephants too!
Piper heard the train whistle,
    and he knew just what to do.

"Can we go? Can we go?
    Can we go?" Piper said.
"Can we go?" he repeated,
    but his mom shook her head.

"Son, I'm so sorry,
    but there's just no way.
The circus costs more
    than a field mouse can pay."

"Then, may I go
    and just look at the tent?"
His mom said, "OK,"
    and so off Piper went.

Racing down Swiss Lane
 and up Gouda Street,
He was moving just like
 there were jets on his feet!

He rounded a corner . . .

And slid to a stop,
  for there right before him
  was the circus big top!

He tried to resist,
but the pull was too great.
And he wondered who'd see him
if he slipped through the gate.

74

He knew it was wrong,
    but he just had to go.
"I'm not stealing," he thought.
    "I'm just 'borrowing' the show."

The bleachers were filled,

so he wandered backstage . . .

And found a red stool
   by the lion's big cage.
"I'll just borrow this stool
   till the circus is through,
And I'll borrow these stilts
   and the bear's tutu too."

BACKSTAGE

The things Piper borrowed?
  Well, who could keep track?
He was turning into
  a kleptomousiac!

Piper snickered and said,
  "It won't hurt anyone.
I'll put it all back
  when I'm done with my fun!"

So he put on the tutu
  and climbed on the stool,
Then danced on the stilts.
  He was feeling soooo cool!

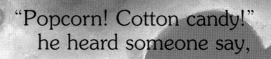
"Popcorn! Cotton candy!"
he heard someone say,

So he leaped from the stilts,
landing right on a tray.

Through a big cloud of pink,
he heard people screaming,
"There's a mouse on that tray!"
How he wished he was dreaming!

There was no place to hide,
  for the bear was now on.
She was bare and quite mad,
  for her tutu was gone!

Her gaze met with Piper's,
  and off that bear went,
Chasing Piper the Mouse
  through the whole circus tent!

It was time for the lions
to enter the ring.
"Where's my stool?!"
yelled the tamer.
"Who's been stealing
our things?!"

While he ranted and raved
'bout the nerve of the louse,
The bear and the lions were
chasing that mouse!

83

The clown entered next,
did a bit of a dance,

But without his big stilts,
he just tripped on his pants!

He joined in the chase,
but he didn't get far.
It's hard to go fast
in a little clown car.

The ringmaster tried
    to regain some control,
But that hyper mouse
    had just stolen the show!

Piper ran for the exit.
    He tried to look back,
But he should've looked straight
    'cause he headed right SMACK . . . .

Into the leg of a
    six-year-old kid,
Who'd been crying because
    of what someone did.

"I was holding two tickets
for my dad and for me,
When someone just took them.
They stole them, you see?"

Piper couldn't believe it!
He was shocked!
He was mad that someone would
steal from this kid and his dad!

88

Then Piper remembered
   the things he had done,
And all of his "borrowing"
   was no longer fun.

Yes, Piper was learning a
   lesson that day.
When you take what's not yours,
   someone still has to pay.

Just then someone called
   out his name, or he thought.
"Piper," he heard,
   "Piper, look what I've got!"

He turned to see who,
   and there by the gate
Was his mom holding tickets.
   "Son, isn't this great!"

"I've just won two tickets
   to the circus today!"

Piper jumped up and down—
"Hip Hip Hooooorra . . ."

Love your neighbor as yourself

But Piper couldn't get that
boy from his mind.
And he knew God would want
him to do something kind.

So he asked Mom's permission.
She nodded, and then . . .

CIRCUS
Admit 1 to have FUN!

Piper gave up his tickets
so they could get in.

The ringmaster praised him!
The audience cheered!
And his mother was beaming
mouse ear to mouse ear!

The clown on his stilts
carried Piper around.
The mayor even named him
"The Mouse of the Town!"

MOUSE
OF
THE
TOWN

Piper danced with the bear,
who now had her tutu,
And rode on the lions,
and when he was through . . .

They asked him to speak.
  Piper said, "Now I know
That this is the way
  a mouse should steal the show!"

BOOK 4

Piper's
Night Before
Christmas

MARK LOWRY
AND MARTHA BOLTON
Illustrated by Kristen Myers

To

Chris, Courtney, Chad, and Chelsea

my nieces and nephews—
not a hyper one in the bunch

They said . . .
It was the night before Christmas,
And all through the house
Not a creature was stirring—
Not even a mouse.

But hours before,
There was much stirring then,
For Piper the Mouse
Was the hyperest he'd been!

He'd tried to be good,
But his patience grew thin.
He wanted it Christmas,
Right there and right then!

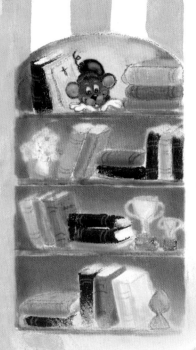

He'd stared at those presents
Like catfish to bait.
What was inside them?
He just couldn't wait!

PIPER

One gift was marked "Piper,"
So trying to peek,
He pulled on the ribbon,
Stretching it with his feet.

But instead of it breaking,
It SNAPPED! with a force,
Catapulting poor Piper
In the air, and of course,
The window was open,
So out Piper flew . . .

There's no telling how many red lights he went through!

Some church doors were open;
He flew right inside—
Past the pews and the pastor—
What a wonderful ride!

Piper landed smack-dab
In a pillow of hay,
Then realized he was now
In their Christmas Eve play!

There was Mary and Joseph
And the shepherds and sheep.
They were saying their lines.
He didn't dare make a peep.

They said that God loved us
And gave us His Son;
So at Christmas it's giving,
Not getting, that's fun!

Piper looked right beside him,
And there on the hay

Lay the most precious baby
Ever born to this day.

Piper jumped off that manger
And ran to his house,
Breaking all the speed limits
That apply to a mouse.

He got his one present
And dragged it four miles . . .

To the church . . .

To the stage . . .

To the manger,
and smiled.

He gave it to Jesus.
It was all he could do.

Then the angel said,
"Jesus would rather have YOU!"

The play was now over.
The cast took their bows.
Piper took one himself
With the sheep and the cows.

Then he walked home that night
With something new to believe,
For he'd learned it's much better
To give than receive.

When he got to his house,
He did not make a peep,
Just made gifts for his loved ones,
Then he fell fast asleep.

So that night before Christmas,
That's why all through the house
Not a creature was stirring,
Not even Piper the mouse!

*"Every good and perfect gift is from above,
coming down from the Father of the
heavenly lights, who does not change
like shifting shadows."*

—James 1:17